'B' is for Bob

E.McL.

First published 2020 by Walker Books Ltd
87 Vauxhall Walk, London SE11 5HJ

2 4 6 8 10 9 7 5 3 1

Text © 2020 Eoin McLaughlin
Illustrations © 2020 Marc Boutavant

The right of Eoin McLaughlin and Marc Boutavant to be identified as author
and illustrator respectively of this work has been asserted by them
in accordance with the Copyright, Designs and Patents Act 1988

This book has been typeset in Clarendon

Printed and bound in China

British Library Cataloguing in Publication Data:
a catalogue record for this book is available from the British Library

ISBN 978-1-4063-7212-0

www.walker.co.uk

not AN ALPHABET BOOK
THE CASE OF THE MISSING CAKE

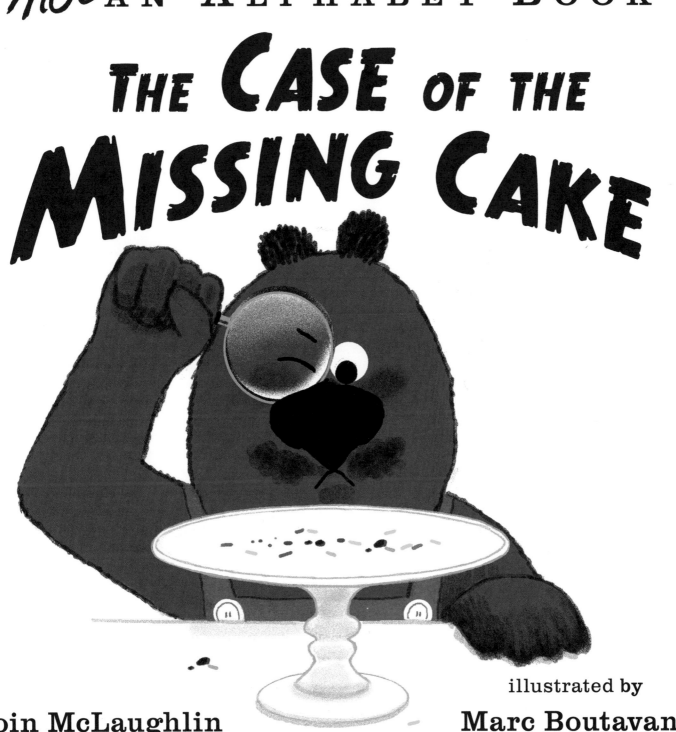

Eoin McLaughlin

illustrated by

Marc Boutavant

WALKER BOOKS
AND SUBSIDIARIES
LONDON · BOSTON · SYDNEY · AUCKLAND

Oh! Thank *goodness* you're here! This was meant to be a simple alphabet book but something **horrible** has happened. The most *terrible* crime! The world's most completely delicious, tongue-jinglingly, chocolaty cake has been ... **STOLEN!**

1

Oh, you should've seen it, it was filled with cream and sprinkled with sprinkles and just sitting on Page 5, but now if you turn there you can see it's

GONE...

Won't you help me find the thief? They're somewhere right here in this book.

2

A is for Apple.

Good day to you, Mr Apple. Did you steal the cake?

Hmmm ... no comment.

B is for Bear.

This is my page. Move along. Nothing to see here.

C is for Cake.

GONE!

D is for Dog.

Are you the cake thief, Dog?

Whimper! No! Just ask the big guy who lives next door. He watches everything I do.

7

E is for Eye.

Hello, you big, creepy Eye. You see everything.

If only you could speak...

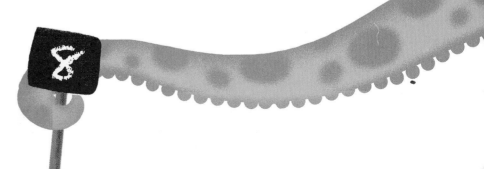

F is for Fox.

You've got a history of stealing sweet treats, Mr Fox. How do you plead?

It was only one tiny bite.
It was years ago.
I'm a different fox now.

G is for Gingerbread Man.

It's true, he bit me.
We all make mistakes, but I forgive Mr Fox.
We're friends now, good friends.

10

H is for Helicopter.

Hmm. Is this how the thief escaped?

I is for Ice cream.

I'll just lick this bit to tidy it up.

12

J is for Jack-in-the-box.

FRIGHT!!! Oh gosh, that blasted thing gets me every time.

13

K is for Kite. L is for Lightning.

Think you're above the law?

You're coming with me, buster.

15

M is for Mermaid.

N is for Nurse.

I just need to lie down for a page.

17

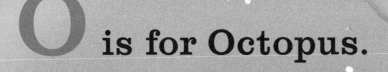

O is for Octopus.

Right! You great big Octopus...

I've seen your huge arms dangling

all over everyone else's pages.

HOW DO YOU PLEAD?!!!

You're looking rather tubby yourself today, Mr Bear. Have you put on weight?

Enough nonsense! It's time for the prime suspect...

18

P is for Pig.

Everyone knows you stole the cake, Pig. You're coming with me to the end of the book. For a big fat punishment.

I'm innocent!
You've got to believe me!
I didn't do it!

Tell it to the Queen, Pig.

19

Q is for Queen.

I caught him, Your Majesty.

Pig, for the crime of eating the cake,
you are banished to Page 27.
FOR EVER!

Oh, please!
Not Page 27!

20

R is for Robot.

Robot, help me escort Pig to Page 27, please.

But I have a wife! I have a family!

21

S is for Sun.

This is the last time you'll see the sunshine for quite some time, Pig.

22

T is for Toothbrush.

Would you like me to brush all the crumbs
out from your teeth again, Bear?

I honestly don't know what you're talking about...

V is for Violin.

This is the end, Pig.

But I'm still young!

25

X is for Xylophone.

Y is for Yogurt.

Don't mind if I do...

Z is for Zip.

Think we've got this case all 'zipped up'.

Aha! Wouldn't you agree, dear reader?

29

What'd'ya mean? You think *I* stole the cake?

I *SAW* you eat it!

OK, you've caught me. I'm guilty. But it was just so completely deliciously, tongue-jinglingly chocolaty, all filled with cream and sprinkled with sprinkles. I just couldn't help myself ...

but this new one will be nice and safe.